Mr. Will Needs to Chill!

Dan Gutman

**Pictures by
Jim Paillot**

HARPER
An Imprint of HarperCollinsPublishers

To Emily Borowicz

My Weirdest School #11: Mr. Will Needs to Chill!

Text copyright © 2018 by Dan Gutman

Illustrations copyright © 2018 by Jim Paillot

All rights reserved. Printed in the United States of America.

www.harpercollinschildrens.com

ISBN 978-0-06-242942-1 (pbk. bdg.)—ISBN 978-0-06-242943-8 (library bdg.)

Typography by Laura Mock

18 19 20 21 22   CG/LSCH   10 9 8 7 6 5 4 3 2 1

First Edition

Contents

The Ding-Dong Man

My name is A.J. and I hate ice cream.

Well, I don't hate *all* ice cream. I like *normal* ice cream, like vanilla, chocolate, strawberry, and mint chip. But my friend Billy, who lives around the corner, told me he likes *weird* ice cream flavors like bacon, garlic, and octopus. What's up with *that*? Why would anybody want to eat octopus-flavored ice cream? What dumbhead dreamed up that idea?

You probably think this book has nothing to do with ice cream, but you're wrong. It has *everything* to do with ice cream.

You see, it was Friday, and we just pledged the allegiance in Mr. Cooper's class like we do every morning. That's when an announcement came over the loudspeaker. It was our principal, Mr. Klutz.

"Good morning, Ella Mentry students," he announced. "It's a sunny day today. Lunch will be sloppy joe sandwiches. There are no birthdays today. The big news is that Mrs. Jafee and I are leaving this morning to go to Principal Camp."

Oh, yeah. Every year, Mr. Klutz and our vice principal, Mrs. Jafee, go hang out in the woods for a few days with a bunch of other principals. Nobody knows why.

"We're going to learn all kinds of new and creative teaching methods to help you kids learn better," said Mr. Klutz.

Oh, so *that's* why they're going to Principal Camp. I wondered who would be our principal while Mr. Klutz and Mrs. Jafee were gone.

"While we're gone," Mr. Klutz continued, "the acting principal will be Dr. Marshall Carbles, the president of the Board of Education."

Oh no! Not Dr. Carbles! He's the meanest man in the history of the world.*

"Have a nice weekend!" announced Mr. Klutz. "I'll see you when I get back from Principal Camp."

---

*If you don't believe me, read *Dr. Carbles Is Losing His Marbles!*

It was hard to focus on reading and writing and math. I kept thinking about mean Dr. Carbles.

It was also hard to focus on reading and writing and math because it's *reading and writing and math*. It would be a lot easier to focus on video games, skateboarding, and football. Too bad we don't study *those* things in school.

Finally it was time for recess, the best part of the day. Me and the gang ran out to the playground to play on the monkey bars. That's when we heard a tinkling sound.

You know the sound I'm talking about?* It's the greatest sound in the world. It's the

---

*No, not that sound! That's *another* tinkling sound.

Ding-Dong truck coming down the street! Everybody stopped what they were doing.

"It's Mr. Will, the Ding-Dong man!" shouted Michael, who never ties his shoes.

"Mr. Will, the Ding-Dong man!" shouted Ryan, who will eat anything, even stuff that isn't food.

"Mr. Will, the Ding-Dong man!" shouted Alexia, this girl who rides a skateboard all the time.

In case you were wondering, everybody was shouting that it was Mr. Will, the Ding-Dong man.

Mr. Will is the greatest man in the world, because he drives the Ding-Dong truck. It's a truck filled with ice cream! What could be greater than that? Anybody who has a truck full of ice cream must be great.

Mr. Will probably gets to eat all the ice cream he wants, every day. Wow! That's my dream job. When I grow up, I'm going to drive an ice cream truck and be a Ding-Dong man.

We ran over to the fence and pressed our faces against it.

"I *love* ice cream," said Andrea Young, this annoying girl with curly brown hair.

"Me too," said Emily, her copycat crybaby friend.

"*Everybody* loves ice cream," said Neil, who we call the nude kid even though he wears clothes.

It was true. Who doesn't love ice cream?

"I can smell the ice cream from here," I said.

"You can't *smell* ice cream, Arlo," said

Andrea, who calls me by my first name because she knows I don't like it. "Ice cream doesn't have a smell."

"It does too."

"Does not."

We went back and forth like that for a while.

"Your *face* has a smell," I told Andrea.

"Oh, snap!" said Ryan.

Mr. Will was playing my favorite song, the Ding-Dong ice cream jingle. It goes like this. . . .

*Do do do do do do do do do do
do do do do do do do do do do*

Or something like that.

Mr. Will plays the Ding-Dong jingle over and over and over, all day long.

"When I was little," Michael told us, "my parents called the Ding-Dong truck 'the music truck.' They said it just drives around all day playing music. They didn't tell me it had ice cream in it."

"*My* parents said that when the music was playing, it meant the Ding-Dong man ran out of ice cream," said Alexia.

"Parents are weird," I said. "They'll do anything to prevent us from eating ice cream."

Mr. Will parked the Ding-Dong truck on the street across from the playground. So near and yet so far away. He leaned out of the truck and waved to us. He was wearing his white Ding-Dong uniform. I really wanted to go over and get some ice cream, but we're not allowed to leave the school grounds during recess. It's not fair!

That's when the most amazing thing in the history of the world happened.

I'm not going to tell you what it was.

Okay, okay, I'll tell you. But you have to read the next chapter. So nah-nah-nah boo-boo on you.

The Great Escape

Suddenly a bunch of our teachers came running out to the playground. In front of all of them was Dr. Carbles.

"What is that racket?" he shouted.

Racket? I didn't see a racket anywhere. Our school doesn't even have tennis courts.

"It's Mr. Will, the Ding-Dong man," somebody said.

"Turn off that horrible noise!" hollered Dr. Carbles. He and the teachers were holding their hands over their ears.

Oh, yeah. The Ding-Dong jingle drives grown-ups crazy. Nobody knows why.

"I can't take it!" shouted Dr. Carbles. "Make that awful music stop!"

It seemed like a good time to start chanting.

"WE WANT ICE CREAM!" I hollered. "WE WANT ICE CREAM!"

I thought the rest of the kids would join in and start chanting with me. But nobody did. I hate when that happens.

"Get that truck out of here!" Dr. Carbles shouted at Mr. Will. "Go peddle your sugary junk food someplace else!"*

Mr. Will stepped out of the Ding-Dong truck and walked slowly toward the fence. Oh, this was going to be good.

"What did you say?" asked Mr. Will.

"Beat it, Ding-Dong man!" shouted Dr. Carbles. "I'll have you arrested!"

"This is a free country," Mr. Will shouted right back. "I can go anywhere I want."

"Turn off that terrible music right *now*!" shouted Dr. Carbles.

"No!" Mr. Will shouted back.

---

*I've heard of pedaling a bike, but it would be weird to pedal ice cream.

The two of them were yelling at each other through the fence. It was awesome. Watching grown-ups argue is fun. And we got to see it live and in person.

"Don't cross me, Ding-Dong man!" shouted Dr. Carbles. "I will make you

regret the day you were born! Nobody messes with me. I'm warning you."

Then he turned around and marched back to school with the other teachers. Mr. Will went back to the Ding-Dong truck. The excitement was over.

We were going to go play on the monkey bars, but we couldn't stop staring at the Ding-Dong truck and thinking about what was inside it.

"I haven't had ice cream in a million hundred years," I said.

"You had ice cream *yesterday*, A.J.," said Michael. "I was over at your house, remember? Your mom made us banana splits."

"Well, it *feels* like that was a million hundred years ago," I said.

"I need ice cream like other people need air," said Ryan.

"I can almost taste it," said Alexia.

"If I don't have ice cream soon, I'm gonna die," said Neil.

"It's not fair," I said. "The ice cream is just sitting right there in the truck, and we can't have it."

If only there was some way to sneak out of the playground. I looked at the bottom of the fence. That's when I got the greatest idea in the history of the world.

"Look," I said. "We can tunnel our way out!"

Everybody looked at the bottom of the fence. It was a few inches off the ground.

"You're right!" said Neil. "Let's dig a

tunnel! A.J., you're a genius!"

I should get the Nobel Prize for that idea. That's a prize they give out to people who don't have bells.

"I don't know," said Andrea. "Digging a tunnel sounds dangerous, Arlo."

"Danger is my middle name," I replied.*

"I'm scared," said Emily, who's scared of everything.

"What if you get caught?" asked Andrea. "You could get in big trouble, Arlo."

"Trouble is my other middle name," I said. "Come on, guys, start digging."

Everybody got down on their hands

---

*It really isn't. But I heard somebody say that in a movie once, and it sounded cool.

and knees and started digging out the dirt under the fence.

"Hurry up," said Ryan. "Dr. Carbles could come back out here any second."

After a million hundred minutes, we dug out enough dirt so I could fit under the fence.

"Okay, wish me luck," I said as I started to slide under.

"Wait a minute," Michael said. "Do you have any money?"

Oh, yeah. Ice cream costs money.

Everybody emptied their pockets. Neil had four pennies. Michael had two quarters. Alexia had a quarter and some dimes. Ryan had some Life Savers. They gave it all to me.

"I don't feel good about this, Arlo," Andrea said.

"A man's gotta do what a man's gotta do," I told her.

"It was nice knowing you, A.J.," said Alexia. She put her hand on my shoulder. I thought she might cry.

"If I don't make it back alive," I told her, "you can have my skateboard, Alexia."

Ryan and Michael pulled up the bottom of the fence a little so I could fit under it.

"I'm going in, guys," I said.

"If you don't make it back, Arlo," said Andrea, "I will always remember you."

"Oooooh!" Ryan said. "Andrea said

she'll always remember A.J. They must be in *love*!"

"When are you gonna get married?" asked Michael.

If those guys weren't my best friends, I would hate them.

I slid under the fence and climbed out the other side. I was free!

Ice Cream Is Ice Cream

I ran over to the Ding-Dong truck and pulled the coins out of my pocket.

"I need ice cream!" I shouted to Mr. Will. "Fast!"

"Well, you came to the right place, A.J.," he replied. "What can I get for you?"

"I'm in a hurry," I said. "I'll just have an ice cream cone."

"Great!" said Mr. Will. "Chocolate or vanilla?"

"Chocolate."

"Soft serve or hard ice cream?" asked Mr. Will.

"Soft."

"Wafer, waffle, or sugar cone?" asked Mr. Will.

"Wafer," I told him. "Can we move this along?"

"Dipped or undipped?" asked Mr. Will.

"Undipped."

"Sprinkles?" asked Mr. Will.

"Sure. Whatever."

"Chocolate or rainbow sprinkles?" asked Mr. Will.

"Rainbow. Either way. I don't care."

"There's just one problem, A.J.," said Mr. Will.

"What's the problem?" I asked.

"I don't have any ice cream cones today."

WHAT?!

"Why didn't you tell me that before?"

"You didn't ask," said Mr. Will.

On the other side of the fence, the gang was shouting for me to hurry up. I looked at the little pictures of ice cream on the side of the Ding-Dong truck.

"Okay," I told Mr. Will. "I'll have a crushed cherry sundae."

"Sorry. I'm all out of those," he replied.

"How about a lemon berry slushie

float?" I asked Mr. Will.

"Just sold the last one."

"Popsicle? Fudgsicle? Creamsicle? Dreamsicle?" I asked Mr. Will.

"Out of stock."

"Milk shake? Ice cream sandwich? Banana boat?"

"Nope."

"Turbo Rocket? Choco Taco? Dip-n-roll?" I asked Mr. Will.

"Not today. Sorry."

I wasn't getting anywhere. Time was running out. Recess would be over soon.

"Well, what kind of ice cream *do* you have?" I asked Mr. Will.

"Let me see . . . ," he said, looking into

the freezer. "How about an octopus Push-Up pop?"

"Octopus?" I said. "Ugh!"

"It's not octopus *flavored*," said Mr. Will. "It just *looks* like an octopus."

"Okay, okay," I said. "I'll take anything. Ice cream is ice cream."

"That will be seventy-nine cents," said Mr. Will.

I'm good at math. I pulled out three quarters and four pennies and gave him the coins. He handed me the octopus Push-Up pop. I started running back to the fence.

But I couldn't resist. I had to take a bite of the Push-Up pop first. I stopped for a second and ripped off the wrapper. The Push-Up pop was a beautiful thing, with red and blue swirls. I was about to take my first bite.

That's when the weirdest thing in the history of the world happened. Suddenly I heard a loud siren and whistles behind me.

"Hands up!" a voice shouted through a bullhorn. "We've got you surrounded!"

I put my hands in the air.

"Drop the Push-Up pop and nobody gets hurt!" the voice shouted.

I turned around. It was Dr. Carbles!

I've seen enough movies in my life to know that when somebody tells you to drop what you have in your hand, you

should always say, "Who's gonna make me?"

"Who's gonna make me?" I asked.

"I am!" shouted Dr. Carbles.

I've seen enough movies in my life to know that when somebody says they're going to make you, you should always say, "You and what army?"

"You and what army?" I asked.

"Me and *this* army," shouted Dr. Carbles.

At that moment, a bunch of big goons in military uniforms came around the corner. They looked mean, and they had some angry, barking dogs with them.

I've seen enough movies in my life to know that when an army actually shows up, you should always shout, "You'll never take me alive!" And then you should make a run for it.

"You'll never take me alive!" I shouted. And then I made a run for it.

I was heading for the hole under the fence.

"Get him, boys!" shouted Dr. Carbles. "Release the dogs!"

I didn't know what to do. I didn't know what to say. I had to think fast.

"Run for your life, A.J.!" shouted Neil.

Everybody was yelling and screaming and shrieking and hooting and hollering and freaking out as I ran back to the fence.

Dr. Carbles's goons and their dogs chased me. They grabbed me just before I got back to the hole we dug.

"Up against the fence, A.J.!" shouted Dr. Carbles. "Step away from the Push-Up pop."

"Okay! Okay! I give up!"

Marshall Law

You probably think Dr. Carbles locked me in a torture chamber and pulled my eyelashes out one at a time and set my toenails on fire. Well, he didn't do any of those things. He just made me write this a hundred times in my notebook. . . .

I will not sneak under the fence and go get ice cream from the Ding-Dong truck. I will not sneak under the fence and go get ice cream from the Ding-Dong truck. . . .

Bummer in the summer! It took me all weekend to finish. My hand hurt! It was the worst weekend of my life. I wanted to go to Antarctica and live with the penguins.

When I got to school on Monday morning, something was different. There was barbed wire across the top of the playground fence. At each corner of the school, there was a guard tower. The guard towers had security cameras and searchlights on them. Mean-looking goons in uniforms were patrolling the playground with attack dogs.

"This is *bad*," said Ryan when I saw him on the front steps.

"It looks like Dr. Carbles is turning our school into a prison," said Neil.

"How do you think he got those guard towers over the weekend?" asked Michael.

"He must have gone to Rent-A-Guard Tower," I guessed. "You can rent anything."

"I hope Mr. Klutz and Mrs. Jafee come back from Principal Camp soon," said Alexia.

We went inside the school and walked a million hundred miles to Mr. Cooper's class. He didn't look happy and excited like he usually does. He just sat at his desk staring off into space. That's when the morning announcements came over the loudspeaker. It was the voice of Dr. Carbles.

"It will be cloudy and depressing today," he announced. "Lunch will be dried mush. There are no birthdays today, or ever again. Birthdays are for losers."

WHAT?!

"Boooooooooooooo!" everybody started shouting.

"There will be *no* sneaking over to the Ding-Dong truck during recess," continued Dr. Carbles. "From now on, recess is canceled. Recess is for losers."

WHAT?!

"Booooooooo!"

"Maybe we can go to the Ding-Dong truck after school lets out this afternoon," Michael whispered hopefully.

"And you can forget about going to the Ding-Dong truck after school lets out," Dr. Carbles announced. "I got a restraining order against Mr. Will. He isn't allowed to come within five hundred feet of the school anymore. So *nobody* gets ice cream. Not on *my* watch."

What did watches have to do with anything? Why would anybody put ice cream on a watch? That would be weird.

"I wonder when we'll be allowed to get

ice cream again," whispered Emily.

"You can forget about getting ice cream for the rest of your *life*," announced Dr. Carbles.

WHAT?!

"Boooooooo!"

"Wow, it's almost as if Dr. Carbles can hear us talking," whispered Andrea.

"I heard that!" said Dr. Carbles. "Mr. Cooper's students had better stop whispering to each other, or they'll all be in big trouble!"

"He put a bug in our classroom!" whispered Andrea.

"Gross!" I shouted, looking inside my desk. "I hate bugs."

"Not *those* kinds of bugs, dumbhead," said Andrea. "Dr. Carbles planted a microphone somewhere in here. He's listening to every word we say."

"That's right," said Dr. Carbles. "So you'd better watch your p's and q's."

Huh? Why should we watch *those* letters? It didn't make any sense.

"I'm afraid," said Emily, who's afraid of everything.

But I was afraid too. We all were.

Finally the morning announcements were finished. I looked over at Mr. Cooper to see what he was going to teach us. But he just sat there with his head on the desk.

"What are we going to work on this

morning, Mr. Cooper?" asked Andrea. "Social studies?"

"No."

"Reading?" asked Alexia.

"Nah."

"Do you want us to turn to page twenty-three in our math books?" asked Ryan.

"Whatever," groaned Mr. Cooper. "I don't care."

That was weird. Mr. Cooper *loves* teaching us stuff.

After a few minutes he told us it was time for fizz ed with Miss Small. Yay! I love fizz ed. We walked a million hundred miles to the gym. When we got there, Miss Small didn't look very happy either. She was sitting on the floor under the basketball hoop.

"Are we going to play basketball this morning, Miss Small?" I asked.

"No."

"Are we going to have relay races?" asked Alexia.

"No. Just go out in the playground and do whatever you want," Miss Small muttered. "I'm not in the mood."

Wow. None of the teachers wanted to teach! With Dr. Carbles in charge, they just looked sad.

So we did what we were told. We went out to the playground. And you'll never believe in a million hundred years what happened next.

There was that sound in the distance.

A jingly-jangly sound.

It was . . . the Ding-Dong truck!

"He's back!" I shouted. "Mr. Will is back!"

"Hooray!" everybody shouted as the Ding-Dong truck pulled up and Mr. Will stepped out of it.

That's when the weirdest thing in the

history of the world happened.

A tank came rolling down the street.

Not a fish tank. It would be weird if a fish tank came rolling down the street. No, it was one of those army tanks, with a cannon in front. I saw it with my own eyes!

Well, it would be pretty hard to see something with somebody *else's* eyes.

The tank stopped close to the Ding-Dong truck. The hatch on the top opened up. And guess whose head popped out of it? Yes, it was Dr. Carbles's!

"You are breaking the law, Ding-Dong man!" he shouted through his bullhorn. "Get out of here, and turn off that horrible music!"

"No way!" Mr. Will shouted back. "Did you ever hear of the First Amendment?

We have freedom of speech in this country, you know!"

"Your freedom of speech ends at my ears!" shouted Dr. Carbles.

"Your students want ice cream!" shouted Mr. Will.

"I don't care what my students want!" Dr. Carbles shouted back. "If you don't get out of here right this minute, I will *make* you leave."

It looked like there was going to be a big fight. Like maybe Mr. Will was going to shoot soft serve ice cream out of a hose on the Ding-Dong truck. That would be cool.

"I don't like violence," said Andrea. "It's

inappropriate for children."

"What do you have against violins?" I asked her.

"Not violins, Arlo! Violence!"

I knew that. I was just yanking Andrea's chain.

But there was no battle. Mr. Will didn't spray Dr. Carbles with ice cream. He just walked back to the Ding-Dong truck and slowly drove away.

"Don't come here again!" Dr. Carbles shouted as he shook his fist in the air at Mr. Will. "I will crush your pathetic ice cream rebellion."

There was nothing we could do but watch through the fence. Dr. Carbles turned around and looked at us.

"Go back to class, you little punks!" he barked.

He's mean! Having Dr. Carbles as our principal was worse than TV Turnoff Week. It was worse than National Poetry Month. It was worse than TV Turnoff Week and National Poetry Month *put together*.

As Mr. Will drove off, we could hear the Ding-Dong jingle fading away in the distance. For the first time ever, it sounded sad and lonely.*

---

*This is the sad part of the book. Get some tissues, will you? You're slobbering all over yourself.

Dried Mush and Cold Gruel

It was really quiet when we got to the vomitorium for lunch that day. Everybody was afraid of what Dr. Carbles might do next.

Me and the gang waited in line until we reached Ms. LaGrange, our lunch lady. Ms. LaGrange is strange. One time, she wrote a secret message in the mashed potatoes. That was weird.

"What's for lunch, Ms. LaGrange?" asked Michael.

"Today I'm serving a bowl of dried mush with a piece of stale bread," she replied sadly.

The mush looked gross.

"Mush is a food?" asked Alexia.

"It is *now*," Ms. LaGrange replied. "I'm under direct orders from Dr. Carbles. And tomorrow we will have cold gruel."

"Gruel? What's that?" asked Neil.

"You don't want to know," Ms. LaGrange replied.

"Can we get dessert?" I asked.

"Dessert?" said Ms. LaGrange with a

snort. "Are you kidding?"

"No dessert?" I asked.

At that moment, a voice came out of a little speaker next to the cash register.

"Dessert is for losers!" said the voice. "Eat your dried mush and stop complaining! You kids are lucky to get any food at all."

It was Dr. Carbles! There was a little video camera next to the cash register.

"I've got my eye on you, A.J.," Dr. Carbles said. "Don't try any funny stuff or you'll be in big trouble."

We found an empty table and sat down. I looked at my bowl of dried mush.

"I'm not eating this," I said.

"Me neither," said everybody else.

Except Ryan, of course. Ryan will eat anything, even stuff that isn't food.

"I'll try it," he said.

Ryan dipped his spoon into the dried mush.

Then he brought the spoon up to his lips.

I was already grossed out.

Then Ryan opened his mouth.

I thought I was gonna die.

Then Ryan put the spoon in his mouth.

Isn't this exciting?*

_____

*Here's a tip for all you writers out there. If you want a story to sound exciting, all you need to do is put each sentence on a line by itself. That's the first rule of being an exciting writer!

Then Ryan swallowed the dried mush. Ugh, gross!

I looked at Ryan. Michael looked at Ryan. Andrea looked at Ryan. Neil looked at Ryan. *Everybody* was looking at Ryan.

"Not bad," Ryan finally said. "It tastes like pudding."

Pudding?! We all dipped our spoons into the dried mush. Actually it wasn't bad once you put some sugar on it.

But even so, everybody was in a bad mood during lunch. Recess had been canceled. After we finished eating, we were told to go out to the playground, where Dr. Carbles was waiting for us.

"Are we going to play a game?" asked

Andrea hopefully.

"No!" barked Dr. Carbles. "Games are for losers. Today you're going to learn how to march."

WHAT?!

"Pringle up!" Dr. Carbles shouted through his bullhorn. "Forward, march! Left! Right! Left! Right!"

It was horrible. Marching is no fun at all. While we were marching back and forth, I looked over to see if the Ding-Dong truck was parked outside the school. It wasn't. Mr. Will was nowhere to be seen.

"Left! Right! Left! Right!" barked Dr. Carbles.

"Where do you think Mr. Will went?"

Michael whispered as we marched.

"Maybe he went to Dirk School," whispered Ryan.

Ugh. Dirk School. That's a school on the other side of town for genius kids. We call it "Dork School."

"Left! Right! Left! Right!"

"Maybe Dr. Carbles kidnapped Mr. Will and tied him up in a dungeon," I whispered. "That stuff happens all the time, you know."

"Stop trying to scare Emily," said Andrea.

"I'm scared," said Emily.

"Left! Right! Left! Right!" barked Dr. Carbles. "Marching makes you *strong*. Playing silly games makes you *weak*."

Dr. Carbles had us marching back and forth across the playground for a million hundred hours. It was horrible.

"I'm not sure I remember what ice cream tastes like anymore," Ryan whispered.

"I think it's cold and wet," whispered Michael.

"I'll never know what an octopus

Push-Up pop tastes like," I said.

"Someday we'll look back on our childhood," whispered Alexia. "We'll tell our grandchildren what ice cream tasted like."

"Those were the good old days," I whispered to Alexia.

"What, you mean yesterday?" whispered Neil.

"Left! Right! Left! Right!"

"Even if we can't eat ice cream anymore," whispered Andrea, "at least we can have frozen yogurt."

"Frozen yogurt isn't ice cream!" I whispered. "It's not the same!"

"You're right, Arlo," Andrea admitted. "Life wouldn't be worth living without ice cream."

That's when Emily started to cry. Then we *all* started crying.

Everybody was whimpering and sniffling and snorting. It was the saddest day in the history of the world.*

---

*Hey, when do the jokes start again? Isn't this book supposed to be funny? You should get your money back! That is, unless you got it from the library. Then it was free anyway.

6

Hooray for Mr. Klutz!

The next day when we got to school, I saw the most amazing thing. The guard towers were gone! The barbed wire was gone! So were the security cameras and the barking dogs! And most importantly, Dr. Carbles was gone! Standing at the top of the front steps and giving everyone hugs was our principal, Mr. Klutz.

He has no hair at all. I mean *none*. His
head is like a bowling ball with a face on it.

"He's back!" everybody was shouting.
"Mr. Klutz is back!"

Mr. Klutz is a nice man. He's not mean
like Dr. Carbles.

"I missed you kids!" Mr. Klutz shouted
when we all came over to hug him.

"We missed you too!" said Emily.

"Dr. Carbles is mean," said Ryan.

"Marshall can be a little . . . uh, strict," Mr. Klutz replied.

"A little?" said Michael. "He drives a *tank* to school."

"Did you have a good time at Principal Camp, Mr. Klutz?" asked Andrea.

"Oh yes," he replied. "Mrs. Jafee and I met lots of experts in the field of education, and we learned all kinds of new ways of teaching. I think it's going to help you kids learn things."

Ugh. Learning things is a drag. But at least it will be better than having mean Dr. Carbles around.

"So we don't have to march in the play-ground anymore?" asked Neil.

"Nope," said Mr. Klutz.

"We don't have to eat dried mush and cold gruel for lunch?" asked Alexia.

"Never again."

"Can we have recess today?" asked Ryan.

"Sure!"

"Can we go out for *ice cream* during recess?" I asked hopefully.

"Why not?" said Mr. Klutz. "In fact, you can go out for ice cream right *now*."

"HUH?" we all said, which is also "HUH" backward.

This was too good to be true! I figured

Mr. Klutz must be pulling a prank on us. We're *never* allowed to eat ice cream first thing in the morning. That's the first rule of being a kid.

"Really?" I asked. "We can have ice cream first thing in the morning?"

"Absolutely!" said Mr. Klutz. "One of the experts at Principal Camp told me that kids learn better when they eat ice cream for breakfast. He said the cold wakes up your brain.*

Hmmm, that makes sense.

"Hooray for Mr. Klutz!" everybody started chanting. "Hooray for Mr. Klutz!"

"Go ahead!" said Mr. Klutz. "I think I

---

*That is a total lie.

hear the Ding-Dong truck coming down the street right *now.*"

He was right! The Ding-Dong truck pulled up across from the school. It was playing the Ding-Dong jingle, as always.

"Ah, I love that song," said Mr. Klutz.

"Mr. Will is back!" somebody shouted.

"Hooray for Mr. Will!" everybody started chanting. "Hooray for Mr. Will!"

"Let's go get ice cream!" Alexia shouted.

"Yeah!"

We were all about to run over to the Ding-Dong truck, but then we stopped.

"Wait," Michael said. "I don't have any money."

"Neither do I," said Emily.

"I just have my lunch money," said Andrea.

"You don't need to use your own money," said Mr. Klutz.

He reached into his pocket and pulled out his wallet. Then he gave each of us a dollar.

What?! Free ice cream? First thing in the morning? This couldn't be happening! It was going to be the greatest day of my life.

We all ran over to the Ding-Dong truck. That's when the most amazing thing in the history of the world happened. The Ding-Dong truck was back, but Mr. Will wasn't inside it! It was some *other* Ding-Dong guy, with blond hair. He was wearing a white Ding-Dong uniform just like Mr. Will.

"Where's Mr. Will?" we all asked him.

"I don't know," the Ding-Dong guy said. "I guess he took the day off. I'm Mr. Bill."

Hmmm, that was weird. Well, I didn't care *what* the guy's name was. As long as he had ice cream.

"Do you have octopus Push-Up pops?" I asked Mr. Bill.

Ever since Dr. Carbles took away my octopus Push-Up pop, I had been thinking about octopus Push-Up pops.

"Sure!" said Mr. Bill as he reached into the freezer and pulled one out. "That will be seventy-nine cents, please."

I handed Mr. Bill the dollar Mr. Klutz gave me. Mr. Bill looked at the dollar bill. He had a puzzled expression on his face.

"I don't know how much change to give you," he said.

What?! That was weird. Mr. Will always gave us our change right away. It didn't even seem like he had to think about it.

"There are a hundred pennies in a dollar," I explained to Mr. Bill. "All you need to do is take seventy-nine from a hundred."

Mr. Bill looked at my dollar bill again. Then he looked at me. He still looked all confused.

"I don't get it," he said. "Can you show me how to do that?"

What?! A Ding-Dong man who can't make change for a dollar? Mr. Bill must be a real dumbhead.

"Uh, I guess so," I said.

He handed me a pad and pencil.

"Look," I told him as I wrote on the pad. "It's simple subtraction. The zero becomes a ten. Ten minus nine equals one. The other zero becomes a nine, and nine minus seven equals two. So you owe me twenty-one cents."

"Ah yes," Mr. Bill said as he handed me two dimes and a penny. "I see it now. Thanks for explaining that to me."

"No problemo," I told him.

I was about to unwrap my octopus Push-Up pop when I stopped.

"Hey," I said, "that sounded a lot like a math lesson just there. Are you a math teacher?"

"No, don't be silly," said Mr. Bill. "I'm just a Ding-Dong man."

Mr. Bill is weird.

Mr. Mill

Mr. Bill's octopus Push-Up pop was yummy. I could hardly taste any octopus at all. Ryan got a coconut Popsicle dip. Michael got a rocket pop. Alexia got a double-dipped butterscotch swirl cone. It was the greatest day of our lives.

When we got inside the school, all the

kids and teachers were smiling again. The day seemed to fly by. Mr. Klutz was right. Eating ice cream first thing in the morning *does* help you learn. At lunchtime in the vomitorium, Ms. LaGrange made yummy chicken nuggets and Tater Tots for us. Everybody was happy.

I must admit, without mean Dr. Carbles around, school was kinda fun. But don't tell the gang I said that. They would never let me hear the end of it.

The next morning, I could hardly wait to get to school. Mr. Klutz was waiting for us on the front steps.

"Can we buy ice cream again today?" Neil asked.

"Of course!" replied Mr. Klutz as he handed each of us a dollar bill. "I can hear the Ding-Dong truck coming down the street right now."

We all ran over to the Ding-Dong truck as soon as it pulled up to the curb. I was expecting to see Mr. Bill, the new Ding-Dong driver guy. But that's when the weirdest thing in the history of the world happened.

Mr. Bill wasn't in the truck! It was some *other* guy. He had red hair.

"Where's Mr. Bill?" we all asked him.

"Mr. Bill is on vacation," said the red-haired guy. "I'm Mr. Mill."

WHAT? How could Mr. Bill be on

vacation already? He just started work yesterday! Oh, well. As long as we get ice cream every morning, I don't care *who* the Ding-Dong guy is.

"I'll have a chocolate Magic Shell Bomb Pop," I told Mr. Mill.

"Sure, coming right up," he replied. "Hey, did you know we've had ice cream as far back as the second century BC?"

"Really?" I asked. "Wouldn't it be rotten by now?"

"No, I mean ice cream was invented a long time ago," Mr. Mill told me. "Alexander the Great liked to eat snow and ice flavored with honey."

"That's nice," I said. "I'll have a chocolate Magic Shell Bomb Pop."

But Mr. Mill didn't give me a chocolate Magic Shell Bomb Pop like I asked. He just kept talking.

"During the Roman Empire," he said, "Emperor Nero sent runners up to the mountains to get snow. Then he had it flavored with fruit."

"That's interesting," I said. "Can I have a chocolate Magic Shell Bomb Pop now, please?"

"Did you know," said Mr. Mill, "that Marco Polo went to the Far East and came back to Italy with a recipe for something that was very much like ice cream?"

"I didn't know that," I said. "Would you *please* give me a chocolate Magic Shell Bomb Pop?"

"By the time the United States became a country, ice cream was really popular," said Mr. Mill. "In fact, George Washington spent two hundred dollars on ice cream during the summer of 1790."

What a snoozefest! Could Mr. Mill possibly be any more boring? All I wanted was to eat some ice cream.

"You don't really *have* any chocolate Magic Shell Bomb Pops, do you?" I asked Mr. Mill.

"Sure I do!" he replied as he reached into the freezer and handed me a chocolate Magic Shell Bomb Pop. "Here you go."

I was about to unwrap my chocolate Magic Shell Bomb Pop when I stopped.

"Hey," I said, "that was sort of a history lesson you just gave me. Are you a history teacher?"

"No, don't be silly," said Mr. Mill. "I'm just a Ding-Dong man."

Mr. Mill is weird.

Mr. Hill

The chocolate Magic Shell Bomb Pop was awesome. I couldn't wait to get to school the next morning so I could get more ice cream from Mr. Mill. We all ran over to the truck as soon as we heard the Ding-Dong jingle.

But Mr. Mill wasn't there. It was some *other* Ding-Dong guy!

"Where's Mr. Mill?" I asked him.

"Mr. Mill is sick today," the new Ding-Dong guy told me. "I'm Mr. Hill. What would you like?"

"Can I have a Ding-Dong double-dipped Dixie Doodle?" I asked.

"Sure, coming right up," said Mr. Hill. "By the way, do you know what ice cream is made out of?"

"No," I told him. "I just like to eat it."

"Ice cream is made out of cream or milk, sugar, and sometimes eggs and flavoring," he told me. "And each molecule of sugar contains twelve carbon atoms, twenty-two hydrogen atoms, and eleven oxygen atoms."

Mr. Hill took out a pad and started drawing a weird picture. . . .

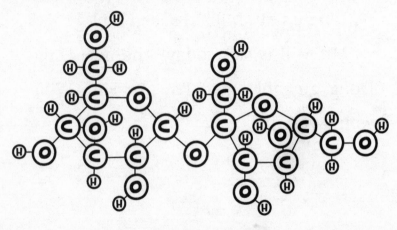

"Nice picture," I said. "Can I have my Ding-Dong double-dipped Dixie Doodle now?"

"After all the ingredients are combined, they get pasteurized," said Mr. Hill. "Do you know what pasteurized means?"

"They leave the ice cream out in a pasture for a while?" I guessed.

"No," said Mr. Hill. "That's when a liquid is heated to a very high temperature to kill off the germs, and blah blah blah blah it is cooled blah blah blah blah Louis Pasteur blah blah blah blah French scientist who invented it blah blah blah blah . . ."

He went on like that for a million hundred minutes. What a snoozefest.

"How about that Ding-Dong double-dipped Dixie Doodle?" I finally asked.

"Pasteur is famous for his discoveries blah blah blah blah helped prevent diseases blah blah blah blah germs blah blah blah . . . ," said Mr. Hill.

I was going to just walk away, but suddenly Mr. Hill stopped blabbing about germs. He reached into the freezer and pulled out a Ding-Dong double-dipped Dixie Doodle for me. I took off the wrapper and had a bite. It was yummy.

"All that stuff you told me about ice cream sounded a lot like science class," I told Mr. Hill. "You're not really a science teacher, are you?"

"No, don't be silly," said Mr. Hill. "I'm just a Ding-Dong man."

Mr. Hill is weird.

9
The Big Surprise Ending

We got free ice cream every day! Chocolate marshmallow. Vanilla fudge ripple. Cookies and cream. You name it. It was the greatest week of my life.

You would think that everybody would have been happy. But when we were eating lunch in the vomitorium on Friday,

Andrea had on her worried face.

"What's the matter?" I asked her. "Did they cancel your clog-dancing class after school today?"

Clog dancing is a dance that plumbers do. Andrea takes classes in *everything* after school so she can show off how good she is. If they gave classes in toenail clipping, she would take that class so she could get better at it.

"I just don't get it," Andrea said. "I don't understand why Mr. Klutz is giving away money so we can buy ice cream. Grown-ups don't just hand out dollar bills to kids. It's not normal."

"I was wondering that myself," said Ryan. "And why is there a different guy driving the Ding-Dong truck every day?"

"Yeah, and why are all the Ding-Dong guys so weird?" asked Michael.

"Maybe they went crazy listening to the Ding-Dong jingle all day," guessed Neil. "It *does* have that effect on grown-ups."

That's it. I couldn't take it anymore. I stood up.

"What is wrong with you people?" I shouted at them. "I can't believe you're complaining. We're getting free ice cream! Every day! First thing in the *morning*! Just enjoy it!"

"I *do* enjoy it, Arlo," said Andrea. "But I'm suspicious. I think these Ding-Dong guys have some kind of a racket going on."

Huh? What did tennis have to do with anything?

"You guys are nuts," I told them. "As long as I get free ice cream every day, I'm happy."

We all went back to eating our lunch.

Nobody said anything for a while.

"But let me ask you *this*, Arlo," Andrea finally said. "What do you think happened to Mr. Will, the first Ding-Dong man? He hasn't been here all week."

Hmmm. Good question. What *did* happen to Mr. Will?

"Yeah," said Neil. "It's like he vanished off the face of the earth."*

"Maybe Mr. Will moved away," guessed Alexia. "Or maybe he got a new Ding-Dong route."

"Maybe he got fired," guessed Neil.

"Maybe he got *kidnapped*," Ryan guessed.

---

*The earth has a face? That's a new one on me.

"Yeah," I said. "Maybe all those Ding-Dong guys are *fake* Ding-Dong guys who wanted jobs with the Ding-Dong company. So they kidnapped Mr. Will, locked him up in a Ding-Dong truck, and pushed the truck over a cliff! That stuff happens all the time, you know."

"Stop trying to scare Emily," said Andrea.

"I'm scared," said Emily.

"Maybe Mr. Will is . . ."

I waited until everybody was looking at me before I finished the sentence.

". . . dead!"

"We've got to *do* something!" Emily shouted. And then she went running out of the room.

Sheesh, get a grip! That girl will fall for *anything.*

But for once in her life, Emily was right. We *did* have to do something. We had to find out what was going on.

After lunch, instead of playing outside during recess, we decided to go to Mr. Klutz's office. If anybody knew what was going on, it would be Mr. Klutz.

We walked down the hall to his office. When we got there, Mr. Klutz was sitting at his desk. He was eating an ice cream sandwich.

"Hey guys!" he said when he saw us. "Have you been enjoying your Ding-Dong ice cream?"

"Yes," Andrea said. "But we're worried about something."

"What is it?" asked Mr. Klutz. "Did the Ding-Dong truck run out of octopus Push-Up pops again?"

"No," said Andrea. "We want to know why there's a different Ding-Dong guy every day. And why are you giving away money to buy ice cream? What's *really* going on?"

Mr. Klutz didn't say anything for a while. It was like he was trying to decide how to respond.

"Okay, I admit it," Mr. Klutz finally said. "Mr. Bill and Mr. Hill and Mr. Mill are not *real* Ding-Dong guys."

"I *knew* it!" Andrea shouted.

"When I was at Principal Camp last week," Mr. Klutz told us, "I found out that kids can learn a lot when they're not in a classroom. You can learn *everywhere*. So I hired teachers to work in the Ding-Dong truck and pretend to be Ding-Dong guys. I thought it would help you learn math, history, science, and other subjects."

"It did help us!" I told him. "I learned lots of new stuff. Did you know that during the Roman Empire, Marco Polo came home and brought ice cream for George Washington's birthday party?"

"I'm not sure that's true, A.J.," said Mr. Klutz.

"Wait a minute," said Andrea. "Bringing in fake Ding-Dong guys is sort of like lying to us, isn't it?"

"Yes," Mr. Klutz admitted quietly. "I suppose you're right."

"Lying isn't nice," Andrea told him. "We're not supposed to tell lies."

"You're right, Andrea," said Mr. Klutz. "But I was trying to help you kids learn. And you did. You got to eat lots of ice cream too. So everybody comes out a winner, right?"

"Well, there's *one* person who didn't come out a winner," said Andrea. "Mr. Will."

"Yeah," Michael said. "Whatever happened to Mr. Will, the *real* Ding-Dong guy?"

"Hmmm," said Mr. Klutz as he stroked his chin.

Men always stroke their chin when they're thinking, even if they don't have a beard. Nobody knows why.

"That's a good question," he said. "I . . . honestly don't know what happened to Mr. Will."

That's when the weirdest thing in the history of the world happened. We heard a sound.

Well, that's not the weird part. We hear sounds all the time. The weird part was that the sound was coming from above, and outside. It was a muffled voice. And the voice was saying, "Help! Help!"

Mr. Klutz went to the window.

"It's coming from the roof!" he shouted. "Follow me!"

We all ran out of his office and climbed up a secret principal staircase that only principals are allowed to climb on.

"Shhh!" whispered Mr. Klutz when he got to the door that opened up onto the roof. "Don't make a racket!"

Huh?

"Why would anybody want to make a racket at a time like this?" I asked. "Are there tennis courts up on the roof? Why is everybody always talking about tennis rackets?"

"Shhh! Quiet, Arlo!" said Andrea.

Mr. Klutz opened the door to the roof with his secret principal key. We stepped out onto the roof.

We were slinking around up there like secret agents. It was cool. Nobody said anything. You could hear a pin drop.

Well, that is, if anybody had pins with them. Who brings pins to school? That would be weird.

But anyway, there was electricity in the air.

Well, not really. If there was electricity in the air, we would have all been electrocuted. And that would hurt!

But it was really exciting. You should have *been* there!

Suddenly we heard that muffled voice again.

"Help!"

We ran over to where the sound was coming from.

And you'll never believe in a million hundred years what we found up on the roof.

Mr. Will!

"WOW!" everybody said, which is *MOM* upside down.

Mr. Will was tied to a chair. His white Ding-Dong uniform was dirty, and his hair was all messed up. He had ice cream dripping down his face, and there were Popsicle sticks on the floor around him.

"Thank goodness you rescued me!" he said.

"What happened, Mr. Will?" Andrea asked as we loosened the ropes that were tied around him.

"It was horrible!" Mr. Will said. "Dr. Carbles was mad at me for parking my truck outside the school every day and for playing the Ding-Dong jingle over and over again. So he and his goons brought me up here and left me here."

"And you've been here all week?" asked Mr. Klutz. "What did you eat?"

"Ice cream!" said Mr. Will. "I had nothing to eat but ice cream for a week."

Wait. What?

We all looked at Mr. Will.

"You had nothing to eat all week except for ice cream?" I asked.

"Yes!" said Mr. Will.

"And that's a bad thing?" asked Ryan.

"Yeah, what's wrong with that?" asked Michael.

"I'd give *anything* to eat ice cream all week," said Alexia.

"That sounds like a perfect week to me," said Andrea.

"I wish I was in *your* shoes," said Ryan.*

Only a grown-up would complain about having to eat ice cream all week.

---

*What did shoes have to do with anything? And why did Ryan want to put on Mr. Will's shoes? They would be too big. Ryan is weird.

Grown-ups are weird.

"I could have *died* up here!" Mr. Will shouted as we helped him to his feet.

Sheesh. What a whiner! If you ask me, Mr. Will needs to chill.

Well, that's pretty much what happened. Maybe Mr. Will will go back to his job driving the Ding-Dong truck. Maybe Dr. Carbles will get thrown in jail for kidnapping him. Maybe they'll start making octopus-flavored ice cream. Maybe we'll start watching our p's and q's instead of the other letters. Maybe a fish tank will come rolling down the street. Maybe Mr. Will is going to shoot soft ice cream out of a hose on the Ding-Dong truck and spray Dr. Carbles's tank with it. Maybe Ryan will start eating dried mush for lunch every day. Maybe it's true that ice cream wakes up your brain. Maybe people will stop talking about tennis rackets. Maybe Ella Mentry School will become a normal school someday.

But it won't be easy!

GUTMA   FLT
GUTMAN, DAN.
MR. WILL NEEDS TO CHILL!.

06/18